One More Cuddle

igloobooks

This igloo book belongs to:

....

igloobooks

Published in 2019
by Igloo Books Ltd, Cottage Farm, Sywell, NN6 0BJ
www.igloobooks.com

GOL002 0519
6 8 10 11 9 7 5
ISBN 978-1-78557-378-1

Illustrated by Suzanne Khushi
Written by Ronne Randall

Designed by Justine Ablett
Edited by Hannah Cather

Printed and manufactured in China

It was evening and outside
the Mouse House, the sun
was going down.

"Come, Little Mouse,"
said Mummy. "Put away
your toys now. It's nearly
time for bed."

"Can't I stay up a bit longer?"
he asked, wiggling his whiskers.
"I don't feel sleepy at all."

Mummy smiled. "A nice, warm,
bubbly bath will help," she said.

Upstairs, water sploshed into the bath and soft, soapy bubbles filled the tub. Mummy helped Little Mouse get in.

splish, splash!

The floaty and foamy bubbles felt nice!

Mummy gave Little Mouse a big cuddle as she wrapped him in a thick, fluffy towel. "Warm and clean, ready for dreams," she said, as she helped him button his cosy pyjamas.

But Little Mouse was still not ready to go to sleep.
"A soothing drink will warm your tummy,"
said Mummy, taking him down to the kitchen.
"Sip it slowly, Little Mouse."

In the living room, Mummy and Little Mouse snuggled up together.
Mummy read Little Mouse a dreamy bedtime story.

Little Mouse loved
the pictures of boats
sailing
on the waves.

When the story was finished,
Mummy took Little Mouse
back upstairs.
"Now it's time for bed,"
she said, gently.

"But I'm still not sleepy,"
said Little Mouse.

"Let's get you tucked up
with Bunny in your cosy bed.
You'll be sleepy soon,"
Mummy promised.

Little Mouse snuggled down under the covers. He cuddled Bunny close. But just a minute later…

… "Mummy, I can't sleep!" he called. "I need a bedtime song!"

In her soft, sweet voice, Mummy sang a gentle lullaby about a beautiful spring garden. Little Mouse's eyelids got heavier and heavier.

"Night night, Little Mouse," whispered Mummy. "Sweet dreams."

Just two minutes later, there was a

pitter-patter, patter-pitter

and Little Mouse came hurrying down the stairs.

"Mummy!" he said. "I STILL can't sleep!
I think I need one more cuddle."

Mummy put her arms around Little Mouse. She gave him a big, soft Mummy cuddle and another one for good measure. She kissed his soft whiskers, too.

"Time to go back to bed now," said Mummy, taking Little Mouse back upstairs. But Little Mouse was still worried.

"I don't think I can fall asleep yet," he said. "What if a monster comes to get me?"

"I will close the curtains to keep you safe," said Mummy.

"Night night, Little Mouse," Mummy said,
as she tucked him in. "Sweet dreams."

Suddenly, Little Mouse sat up.
"But what if I DON'T have
sweet dreams?" he asked.

Mummy switched on Little Mouse's starry night light.

"Just wish on your special star for
sweet dreams," she said. "Bunny will stay
close by while you're sleeping."

So, Little Mouse snuggled under the covers and wished on his star for sweet dreams.

He wished for dreams about brave adventures with Bunny…

… and dreams about bright, sunny gardens…

… and dreams about soft, whiskery kisses from Mummy.

Soon, Little Mouse's eyelids drooped and
drooped… and drooped some more…
and closed tight.

At last, Little Mouse was fast asleep.

And so was Mummy!

Night night and sweet dreams, Little Mouse… and Mummy!